CANCELLED BY THE CARTEL

A HEROES COLLECTION SHORT STORY

ALEXANDRIA BLAELOCK

BlueMere Books
MELBOURNE, AUSTRALIA

For permission requests, please contact
enquiries@bluemerebooks.com.

Ordering Information:
Discounts are available on quantity purchases. For details, contact orders@bluemerebooks.com.

Cancelled by the Cartel/Alexandria Blaelock
paperback ISBN: 978-1-922744-29-6
digital ISBN: 978-1-922744-30-2

CANCELLED BY THE CARTEL

Daisy Day paced the length of the faded green paisley carpet, her black patent heels thudding through what was left of the pile to echo in the sparsely furnished office.

She'd inherited the mahogany bookshelves, filing cabinets, desk and chairs along with the Director's Office from her predecessor, but he'd taken all the contents with him, and she saw no need for the fripperies fat old white men favour.

She theorised they enjoyed watching their secretaries dust them while they fumbled with their belts under the desks.

Her secretary, the young Miss Hawkins, had more important things to do than dust her baubles while she watched.

She realised she was smoothing the rough fabric of her navy-blue tweed suit in an attempt to hold the stress at bay and forced herself to fold her hands behind her back.

Yes, this week's Monday morning meeting was a BIG meeting with the new Department Head, but she was as prepared as she was ever going to be. All the files revised, all the problems highlighted, everything tickety-boo.

After a smart about-turn, she paced the length of the carpet again and picking up her lukewarm tea, looked out the window.

It was the kind of crisp, bright blue mid-winter day that teased you with the prospect of being warmer outside than it really was. She could almost smell a floral-scented breeze, though of course, you didn't get that in Summer in Melbourne let alone the Winter.

She held the saucer in her left hand, a little under her chin, and sipped from the cup in her right. Her fingers curled into her palm, balancing the weight.

None of that mucky-muck little fingers raised for her.

Pigeons circling in the nameless small park across the street carved shadow arcs across the faded blue and white floral wallpaper.

At least until some kind of falcon swooped and they scattered.

Raised voices in the corridor approached the door.

She cocked her head, Hawkins attempting to deflect Mr Pomfrey.

She sighed. And so it began.

Really, she was too old for this. She ought to retire and take a place out in the countryside. Get a dog and take it for long country walks.

Certainly, this was not the life she'd imagined when she was young.

She'd expected marriage and children. Greeting Don with his pipe and slippers when he returned from a hard day at the office.

And yet he'd been murdered in front of her.

Well, not actually in front of her. She'd been unconscious thanks to a sharp blow on the head, and who knew how long he'd survived after that.

Or what had been done to him.

She'd woken up in hospital several days later.

She could still remember the scent that preceded the blow; fog or more likely mist rising from the river, cigar smoke, supple leather, whisky and some kind of creamy shaving soap.

And now, like Miss Marple, she was a spinster; old and marginally relevant. Though having skipped the children and decades of Sunday dinners, still with her svelte shape intact.

She put the tea back on her desk and smoothed her hand across her immaculate salt and pepper chignon as she sat. Slipping her glasses on as she picked up a sheaf of papers to look busy.

The knock came almost before she was ready for it, and Pomfrey burst in before she acknowledged it. Followed by the distraught secretary.

Mercifully Pomfrey fell silent at her mildly reproving look. Over her spectacles and under her slightly frowning brow.

The older woman's weapon is to send grown men back to their childhoods with a disapproving face.

"I'm sorry Ma'am," Hawkins said, "Mr Pomfrey insisted."

Daisy waved her away with a small smile so she would know she wasn't to blame. The girl nodded, and leaving the door open, retreated to her desk outside the door.

"Pomfrey, why don't you take a seat?" she put her papers down, indicated the seats in front of her desk, and folded her hands.

The previous, Director had been a short man who'd sawn an inch or so off the chair legs, and Daisy hadn't seen a reason to swap them out.

With a name like Daisy Day, it had been hard enough to build credibility and rise to the rank of Section Chief, but she still needed all the help she could get when it came to dealing with patronising subordinates like Pomfrey.

He spluttered, knowing all about the chair situation. He'd been the kind of crony who'd enjoyed being in on the joke.

Daisy relaxed back into her chair, crossing one leg over the other.

Knowing he couldn't prevent himself from watching, she steepled her fingers under her chin and gently swung her top leg.

Waiting.

The man made a sound of annoyance and threw himself into a chair.

"I want to know what you're going to do about Soho."

Daisy considered his florid, too many drinks over too much lunch face and physique, the cigarette burn in his unfashionable tie, and his greasy Clarke Gable inspired side part with a pencil-thin moustache.

Should she humour him?

No. There were bigger fish to fry now.

Abruptly, she was annoyed with herself as well as him. She was better than him by a long shot.

She dropped both feel to the floor at sat up at her desk.

"That's no longer your concern."

She let his tirade wash over her while she considered what she was in fact going to do about Soho.

And Lord knew how it had become her problem when it was Pomfrey's bad judgement that brought them to this impasse.

Couldn't let him muck it up any further.

She stood up.

"That will do I should think. You've had your say, and I'll take it on board.

"Now," she rested her palms on the desk, stood up, leaning slightly to pick up her files for the meeting, allowing him to imagine cleavage through her high collared suit.

God, she was doing it without thinking. Men like Pomfrey were so easy to manipulate.

"I believe you have other matters to attend to, as do I."

It looked like he was planning to stay and argue some more, so she walked around her desk and gestured towards the door.

He shot out of his chair, clearly set on haranguing her all the way to wherever she was going, but at least he'd left the office.

She made a show of locking the door and pocketing the key, before walking away at a pace she knew he couldn't keep up with.

When exactly was it that handsome young men turned into ageing Pomfreys?

And why was it, that the more repulsive they became, the more voracious their appetites.

Taking the stairs, she left him wheezing in her wake, and two stories up he'd given up.

She took the opportunity to visit the ladies toilet; there were only two in the building, converted by replacing the male sign from the door with a female one.

She gave herself a thumbs-up sign in the mirror, adjusted the lie of her suit and moved on.

It seemed that the main reason for the Monday meeting was to compare notes about their weekend conquests. For the men in the room to detail their exploits in an attempt to embarrass her.

She didn't expect much aside from a couple of wasted hours. Nothing seemed to change, nothing seemed to get done, nothing really happened. Always the same meeting, regardless of new weeks or new faces.

It was possible they were playing her. Then again, they were complacent. Always thinking women were incompetent and easily bullied into submission.

When the Police Investigation into Don's death had stalled, or more likely, swept under the carpet, they'd told her to let it go and move on. They assured her she'd find another beau.

As if you could easily substitute one man with another and not tell the difference.

She hadn't been reassured, and she didn't want another beau, so she'd started her own investigation.

Astounded by what she'd found.

The lines of power and corruption seeped through Parliament, the public service, business and education.

Like any good business, the cartel took an early interest in bright young men and groomed them well.

All those jaded Pomfreys were once young men with stars in their eyes. Lured with a little dabble in this and a flirt with that, just enough to keep them eager and pliant.

Bending the rules a little, led to bending them a lot, until they were so compromised, they had nowhere to turn.

And those that fought back, like Don, left for dead on the way.

She couldn't believe they were so brazen, but at the same time, couldn't quite believe they weren't suspicious of her in the slightest.

Was it because she was a woman, therefore of no account, or that it was simple to arrange an "accident" and eliminate her on short notice?

Must be the bright, starry-eyed men who did that.

The Monday meeting was in the Department Head's office, with the other three Section Chiefs.

His office was similar to her own, only larger, with less filing cabinets and more knick-knacks.

And this week, two chairs behind the desk as well as the four in the front.

Not caring to contribute to the weekend conversation she reviewed her files, and tried to guess what either of the Heads might want to know.

Probably nothing going by other weeks. Either way, they were content for her to fix it and move on, or screw it up and take the fall.

And then Daisy smelled a familiar scent.

One she hadn't realised until that moment she'd been searching for across decades.

And suddenly she was back there by the Yarra River. Walking hand in hand along Flinders Walk. Convinced Don was about to propose to her.

Leaving her head bowed, she shut her eyes.

Could she be wrong about the scent?

She concentrated.

Creamy shaving soap? Check.

Cigar smoke? Check

Whisky? Check

The lack of river mist and leather could be down to meeting indoors rather than by the river.

Not enough to go on, she'd have to give him the benefit of the doubt.

She opened her eyes and watched the other section chiefs greeting him like a long-lost friend.

He was taller and thinner than them, dressed in an immaculately tailored charcoal suit, and possibly handmade black shoes as well.

Blond hair turning grey, grey eyes, clean-shaven, with an easy manner about him.

As his attention turned to her, she stood up.

Not a flicker of recognition.

A moment of sexual interest, gone almost as soon as it registered.

Could she use that to find out more about him? Like was he near the Yarra on that day?

The outgoing chief introduced her to the incoming.

"Miss Day, may I present Mr Carmichael. Carmichael, this is Daisy Day, Section Chief of Planning."

His hand was cool and dry as he enclosed hers within it.

"Miss Day."

"Mr Carmichael."

He turned away, effectively dismissing her as everyone else did.

"Please sit down everyone, I'll just be observing this meeting."

He picked up one of the chairs from behind the desk, and moved it a little way back and across, outside of the circle of chairs. Then leant back to pick a chestnut leather-bound notebook and a black and gold marbled fountain pen from the desk.

As the others began their weekly reports, Daisy looked at him from the corner of her eyes. He appeared intent on taking notes about the matters under discussion.

She took her own notes as the meeting progressed, but now as boredom set in, stole glances at him.

Sometimes she caught him boldly watching her and looked away.

Sometimes he caught her watching him, and she looked away then too.

That he looked at her, made her uncomfortable.

Not because it was sexual, though it was that too, but because he wasn't *overlooking* her.

She gave her report, and he didn't look at the walls or ceiling or carpet. He *looked* at her.

And she wasn't used to that at all.

After the meeting, she attempted her usual early exit, but Mr Carmichael blocked her exit, catching her arm.

She looked at his long, slim fingers circling her arm, and when he didn't withdraw them, glared up at him and wrenched her arm away.

He didn't let go.

"There's something about you Miss Day that makes me uneasy, and I intend to find out what it is."

"I expect you've been a naughty boy and I remind you of Nanny," she replied.

"Now, if you will excuse me, I have more pressing matters than your curiosity to attend to." She attempted to brush his hand loose.

He waited long enough for her to understand he'd let her go.

This time.

Next time, perhaps not.

Daisy left the room, back straighter than a poker, aware he was watching her.

Taking the stairs down, she knew that unlike Pomfrey, it would be damn near impossible to outrun him on the stairs.

Back in the relative safety of her own office, she folded her arms across her chest and looked out the window.

She could feel her heart pounding furiously in her chest.

Was it possible he recognised her from that night on the Yarra?

Conceivably whoever knocked her out had rolled over to check her pulse or that she was truly out of it and not faking.

She'd always assumed she'd been knocked out and left for dead, but was it possible something else happened to her while she was unconscious?

The thought made her shiver.

It had been days before she woke up in the hospital, had the cartel reached into the hospital to ensure she didn't wake up any sooner?

That any evidence from the river bank had been safely removed from her body as well as her clothes?

Or had she got it wrong, was she perhaps not supposed to wake up at all.

She shivered again.

Pacing her office wasn't going to cut this level of stress, she needed to walk it out.

There were some files to be delivered to another Department on the other side of the City. It might be a good idea to deliver them herself.

Maybe take a long walk by the Yarra to see that that kindled any further memories.

She put her coat on, told Hawkins where she was going and set off.

As she exited the building and started walking down the street, she felt her skin crawl.

There was nothing to hide, she didn't look back, yet the feeling someone was watching, or even worse following her, didn't subside.

She set a pace, just this side of a trot in case any Pomfreys were following her.

She dropped off the files, bought a drink she didn't want to drink and a sandwich she didn't want to eat to explain the pause, and sat on a bench by the river.

Quite close to where she'd been knocked out, about midway between the Princes and Queens Street bridges.

On an ordinary day, the slow-moving Yarra was calming.

Sunshine breaking randomly through the clouds. The occasional sound of a tourist boat's motor and horn as it puttered up or down the river, followed by a whiff of diesel. Swiftly diluted by the light breeze blowing upriver.

Today, it seemed one hundred and one seagulls squabbled on its surface. One thousand and one tourists took pictures or ate and drank in the restaurants lining the river's edge.

And unsurprisingly, Mr Carmichael seating himself beside her, sliding his arms along the bench, one almost touching the back of her neck.

"I thought I might find you here."

The hair on the back of her neck was standing on end, but she couldn't let him see how rattled she was, so she slid a little forward and away from his hand, opened her sandwich, and bit into it.

Managing not to spill any of it into her lap.

"Why of all the possible places in the City you might go, did you come here."

Still chewing, she gestured behind her.

He looked over his shoulder at the building behind her, its Departmental logo loud and proud across the facade.

She swallowed, "why are you following me."

He crossed one leg over the other, and gently swung it, much the same as she'd done to Pomfrey earlier that day, she looked at it like it was a tiger snake preparing to strike.

"I'm not following you," he said, "I have a meeting back there in about ten minutes."

There was nothing she could say to that, it had been her argument after all. She took another bite of her sandwich, knowing she couldn't ask him to leave without arousing his suspicion.

Knowing ordinary people didn't throw out lunches they'd barely eaten.

He sat in silence as she ate, lightly tapping the bench behind her with his fingers, leg still idly swinging.

Each mouthful was harder and harder to chew and swallow.

"It *is* a beautiful day by the river," he said, "it's a shame to go back to the office."

He edged a little closer to her, "what say we play hooky and go for a drink instead."

She edged a little further away, "what say we don't."

He looked at her and smiled, a genuine smile, so full of humour she almost forgot he could well be the person who killed her Don.

"You'd sentence me to the drudgery of another meeting after you couldn't wait to get out of the last?"

She choked on her sandwich and couldn't stop coughing. He patted her back and offered her a handkerchief for the tears streaming down her face.

She put the sandwich back into the paper in her lap, and found the napkin in her pocket, just in time to catch the food as it left her mouth.

Gasping for air.

He didn't stop patting her back, so she slid a little closer to the edge of the seat.

"Mr Carmichael. It's really not appropriate for you to be touching me during working hours."

His hand lay still on her back, burning through the thick wool of her overcoat. He leaned in, his scent strong in the close contact, "and after hours?"

"You're my boss, it's not appropriate ever."

"That's right," he said, "and I have a meeting to go to."

He stood up and grasped her shoulder firmly, but not painfully, "I'll be seeing you," then tapped her shoulder three times for good measure before he walked away.

Daisy sat on the bench, watching the river flow by.

Trying to decide whether he was flirting with her, or warning her.

Did he know something? Was he punching her buttons by design or coincidence?

Or did he just think she was an attractive and available female?

One night stand. Doubtful he wanted something longer term.

She scrubbed her face with her hands and sighed. There's a fine line between acceptable behaviour and harassment, sometimes impossible for both sides to navigate.

She sighed and looked at the sandwich in her lap. She hadn't wanted it before, and she definitely didn't want it now. And as for a "drink," well she could do with a shot of hard liquor right now too.

But not here where Carmichael, damn the man, might see.

She folded the paper back around what was left of her sandwich, dumped it in the closest bin, and started retracing her steps back to the office.

She paused outside her favourite bar for a long moment but pushed on back to work. She might need a drink right now, but she needed her wits about her more.

Her Pomfrey-evading tactics weren't going to work on Carmichael.

The rest of the day passed uneventfully, aside from expecting Carmichael to drop by and jumping every time there was a knock on the door.

By the time she'd reached the end of the day she was wound so tight she thought she might explode.

She took the train home and thought she saw him sitting in the next carriage.

Shopping for something for dinner at the supermarket, she thought she saw him at the meat counter.

And at her apartment building, as the lift door slid closed, a hand reached in triggering the safety and reopening the doors to reveal Mr Carmichael.

She looked up at his attractive, smiling face and couldn't quite grasp why he was there in her apartment building.

"Ah Miss Day," he said, "do you live in this apartment building too?"

She could only stare at him, eyes wide, jaw dropping.

"I've just moved back to Melbourne," he continued, "it'll be nice to know someone else here."

He turned to punch the button for his floor, and then turned back, "how wonderful, we're both on the fourth floor!"

Snap out of it NOW, she begged herself.

Somehow, she managed to stand upright, close her mouth and smile a straight lipped smile, "I'm not sure I would go so far as to say we know each other."

"Are you sure? You seem so familiar. I'm sure I've met you before."

"I'm sure I would remember you, and I don't."

He took a step closer, suddenly serious, "are you quite sure. Why don't you think back and tell me where we met?"

Daisy managed not to shrink back, "quite sure."

The lift dinged their arrival at the floor, and she took the opportunity to brush past him and walk to the end of the corridor where her flat was located.

"Oh look," he said catching up with her as she unlocked her door, "we're neighbours."

She opened her door and somehow managed not to slam it.

Dumping her shopping in the corridor, she went straight for the whisky bottle and got herself a large drink.

It seemed that in the space of eight hours, her life had turned to complete chaos through the introduction of Mr Carmichael.

He'd invaded her work, and by moving into the apartment next door, he'd invaded her personal life too.

By now, she was convinced he'd tried to kill her all those years ago. There were just too many coincidences for his appearance to be random happenstance.

The spectre of this had hung over her entire adult life, and now they wanted to ruin the small measure of peace she'd achieved.

She needed to choose; fight or flight?

She had a plan to disappear; cash and traveller's cheques secured in a small safe in her wardrobe. A bag was packed with a few clothes.

But now the time had arrived, and she was annoyed they thought they could bully her into submission.

As the rage moved through her body, she clenched her fists and bared her teeth. An edgy, twitchy feeling rose within her, and planting her feet wide apart, she roared with rage.

It wasn't fair.

She deserved the life that had been stolen from her, and she was damned if Mr Carmichael was going to steal this one too.

She'd always been upright and honest in her all dealings.

Never so much as accepting a glass of water from her clients, never rounding her time sheets up or down, never doing anything that might put her under obligation to another.

It was enough now.

It was time to end this once and for all.

To bring justice, not just for herself, but for all the others the cartel had brought low.

For the first time, she acknowledged to herself that she had been damaged by Don's death. That it was a gaping wound she had never got over.

If she wanted to live an ordinary life, she would have to heal that wound.

Even if she had to die trying.

And then she thought again.

Maybe it was simpler than that.

Maybe the answer was marketing.

Divide and conquer. Twitter campaigns. Cancel culture. Conspiracy theories.

Public Relations is, after all the best defence.

But she had to be clever about it.

She jumped when someone knocked on her door, though it sounded more like someone was beating on it with their fist.

She stepped over the shopping to open it.

"Oh thank God," Mr Carmichael said, "I thought something had happened when you screamed like that. I was going to get the Building Manager to open your door when you didn't answer."

She looked at him blankly. Noticing he had changed into jeans and a powder blue jumper that suited his colouring and brought a touch of colour to his eyes.

He put his hand on his heart, in what she thought was dramatic irony. "I was worried."

And then she understood.

It was all part of his campaign of destabilisation.

And she wondered how she might use this against him.

"It's been a tough day," she said, "would you consider a drink on the rooftop garden?"

"Oh," he said, caught off guard, "okay, sure."

"Let me get changed, and I'll meet you up there in fifteen minutes or so."

He backed up, away from the door. "Sure. Okay. I'll see you there."

She shut the door in his face.

Picking up her shopping, she dropped it in the kitchen on her way to her bedroom. Quickly changed into jeans and an old sweatshirt with a faded logo, then washed her face, pulled the pins from her chignon and combed her hair out with her fingers.

That felt better already.

She prepped some snacks and tossed them in an esky with a half-empty bottle of whisky.

Daisy wasn't sure what she hoped to achieve by inviting him to the roof. It wasn't like she could ask him if he'd killed her boyfriend twenty years ago.

She'd just have to play it by ear.

She arrived early, but he'd arrived earlier and spread his own picnic on the communal table closest to the edge of the roof.

The one behind the largest pot plants, that offered the greatest measure of privacy.

Fortunately, he'd remembered to bring glasses.

She knocked the first one back, breathing out the fumes.

It left a warm glow in her belly along with a dash of false bravado.

"That bad was it?" he asked, pouring her another drink.

She leant on the railing and looked at the ground. "There's this new guy at work, and the way that he follows me around gives me the creeps."

"Ah," he joined her at the railing. "Well, about that. I'm sure I know you from somewhere."

She swirled the drink around in her glass, "and what if you were doing something wicked at the time?"

"I'm fairly sure I have never done anything wicked."

She sipped her drink, and turned her back to the railing to look at him, "nothing you'd be ashamed to be seen in the newspapers for?"

"Nothing," he said emphatically.

"We'll see," she muttered.

"Sorry?" he leaned towards her

"Nothing.

"Hold this," she said, holding out her glass.

She pulled a hair elastic from her pocket and pulled her hair back into a ponytail. She hadn't intended to show him her scar, but as she turned her head, light glanced across the white threads marking her skin.

"Wait!"

He caught her arm and pulled her back into the light, exploring the web of scarring with gentle fingers.

Surprised, and angry, she pushed him back with both hands on his chest, and he fell into the parapet around the edge of the roof.

He flailed his arms, trying not to drop the glasses and leant on the rails as he tried to get back on his feet. But the railing broke and he started to overbalance.

For an instant she was frozen in place, not wanting to let him fall, and not wanting to save his life.

He let out a strangled cry, and she realised that no matter what he'd done, he didn't deserve to fall six storeys to the ground.

She reached out to take his hand, but he'd already lost his footing and was trying not to fall from the roof.

She lunged at him and managed to catch an arm as he overbalanced, falling to her knees and bracing herself against the concrete gutter.

He swung his other arm and managed to catch hold of the gutter.

"Hold on," she cried.

She tried pulling him further up, but couldn't shift him.

"You have to find a toehold or something to leverage yourself up."

"I can't."

"Don't be stupid. I can't hold you, and if you don't, you'll fall!"

"I can't."

She took a deep breath and held it, speaking through her gritted teeth, "there is no one here but you and me.

"No one is going to turn up in the nick of time to save you.

"The only person who can save you is you."

"I can't."

"You are the worst fucking evil bastard that ever walked this earth," she screamed, "and it would serve you right if I just let you go."

She braced herself, "in fact I'm going to let you go right now."

"Nooooo," he wailed, and finally she heard him scrabbling his feet against the wall of the building.

And suddenly he found a toe hold and launched himself up and over the gutter.

She was too slow to get out of the way, and he landed on her, rolling them both away from the edge, and coming to rest, lying by her side.

Both panting from the exertion.

"I know where I know you from now."

She didn't respond.

"I found you unconscious by the Yarra and called an ambulance. I went with you to the

Royal Melbourne Hospital emergency department."

She turned her head to look at him.

"I waited while they operated on you, and put you into a coma. I only left you because I had a flight to catch, and when I got back, you'd gone."

"What about Don?"

"Don? Who's Don?"

"He was my boyfriend who turned up dead."

He turned to look at her, "you were on your own. No one else was with you."

Daisy looked up at the sky. That changed things a bit.

Had Don been part of the cartel?

Had *he* been the one who bludgeoned her?

Had she been wrong about him all along?

And to cap it all, had he actually died?

"Anyway, I'm glad you made a full recovery."

She looked at him again, "yeah, I'm fine aside from 20 years of excess baggage."

He snorted, "I think I need a drink."

"Sounds good to me. Can you get up?"

He groaned as he elbowed himself to a sitting position, and groaned some more as he used a pot plant to pull himself upright.

He stood swaying, then offered her his hand, "I'm sorry if I came on too strong today."

She took his hand and he pulled her upright, she stumbled as she overbalanced into him.

"Oop," she said, "I thought you might have been the person who murdered Don."

"Ah, that explains your initial reaction. "What gave you the idea?"

"Your cologne."

He let her loose. "I'm afraid we lost the glasses, care to share the bottle?" he offered it to her first.

She sat down and took a swallow, making a guttural noise as the alcohol hit the back of her throat, and offering him the bottle back.

He sat down, looking out over the night sky, bottle dangling between his legs. "What now?"

"I'm sorry I pushed you."

"Not your fault the railing chose that moment to fail."

She sighed, "I don't know what to think anymore. The hatred I felt for the people who murdered Don has controlled me for too long, yet I can't see another way to look at it all."

He took another swig of the bottle and handed it back to her. "What will you do?"

"Just keep going. Get up and go to work, and pretend like it's another ordinary day."

"No need to rush. Take a day off."

"Shouldn't that be my line? You're the one who's just had a near-death experience."

"Maybe we should take a day at the beach. Wash our cares away."

"It's the middle of winter!"
"Best time. No one there."
He grinned, and she started laughing.
And didn't stop for a long time.

THE END

ABOUT THE AUTHOR

Alexandria Blaelock writes stories, some of them for *Ellery Queen's Mystery Magazine* and *Pulphouse Fiction Magazine*. She's also written four self-help books applying business techniques to personal matters like getting dressed, cleaning house, and feeding your friends.

As a recovering Project Manager, she's probably too fond of sticking to plan. She lives in a forest because she enjoys birdsong, the scent of gum leaves and the sun on her face. When not telecommuting to parallel universes from her Melbourne based imagination, she watches K-dramas, talks to animals, and drinks Campari. At the same time.

Discover more at www.alexandriablaelock.com.

BOOKS BY
ALEXANDRIA BLAELOCK

SHORT STORY COLLECTIONS

The Histories of Hayward Hall
Lovelorn, Lovestruck and Love at First Sight
Common or Garden Variety Heroes
Case Files of the Wilkinson Detective Agency
Unavoidable Fates
Christmas Travesties
Five Faces of Felicia Clarke

OTHER FICTION

That Love Nonsense

MS BLAELOCK'S BOOKS

Stress Free Dinner Parties
Signature Wardrobe Planning
Holistic Personal Finance
Minimally Viable Housekeeping
Planning a Life Worth Living

SELECTED SHORT STORIES

Alma's Grace
Balancing the Book
Carmelita Basingstoke
Fate in Your Hands
Kiss of Death
Lady of the Looking Glass
Life in the Security Directorate
Long Weekend in the Snow
Love in the Past Tense
Love in the Security Directorate
Morning Star, Evening Star, Superstar
Needy Bitch
Payton's Run
Phoenix Child
Secret Singer
Shining Star
Ship in a Bottle
Simone Says Hands in the Air
Special Relativity in Space
The Bygone Boyfriend
The Day the Schedule Broke
The Ghost Detectors
The Guardian's Vigil
The Mince Pie Mystery
The Mystery of the Master Suite
The Pseudonym's Bride
The Shadow Thieves
The Time-Space Paradox
Toy Soldiers

www.ingramcontent.com/pod-product-compliance
Lightning Source LLC
Chambersburg PA
CBHW030813190726
48285CB00003B/1169